Series 401
A Ladybird Book

Young children will delight in the adventures of Sandy, the pet rabbit, who runs away to join Bobbity, the wild rabbit, and all his woodland friends.

THE RUNAWAY

Story and illustrations by
A. J. MACGREGOR

Verses by
W. PERRING

Ladybird Books Loughborough

Sandy gazed upon the rabbits,
    Playing blithely in the sun:
Sandy's little heart was breaking,
    "Why," he thought, "can't I have fun?"

"Why should I be here forgotten,
    In this prison rabbit hutch?"
—Sandy's tears were flowing faster,
    But it didn't help him much!

Down among the happy rabbits,

    Someone noticed Sandy's plight:

Bobbity was touched with pity,

    Came along to set things right.

Bobbity said " No more weeping !

Soon we'll have you out of that ! "

Pulled and struggled hard, but Sandy

Seemed to be a little fat !

Michael, Sandy's little master,

    Having mixed the milk and bran,

Came towards them. Rather frightened,

    Bobbity just turned and ran !

Off he sped, away to freedom,

    Through the fence and down the hill,

Leaving Sandy to his master,

    Just a lonely prisoner still!

Michael, who had noticed nothing,
　　Meant to put the bowl inside:
Opened up the hutch, and Sandy
　　Darted out: then Michael cried,

" Sandy! Sandy! Naughty Sandy!
　　Now you've spilt your lovely tea!
Come back here, at once! This minute!! "
　　Sandy didn't stay to see!

Hop, skip, hoppity! went Sandy,

As the bowl went tumbling down:

Michael looked his last on Sandy,

Bobbing tail, and flash of brown!

Down the hill and through the woodland
Scampered Sandy, free at last,
Thought no more of little Michael,
And his rabbit-hutchy past!

Made a bee-line for the warren,
There his furry friends to find:
Didn't think that lonely Michael
Hadn't meant to be unkind.

Sandy found a funny notice,
　　Thought it didn't matter much,
Read " Beware the Fox! " and *giggled*—
　　Silly rabbit from a hutch!

But when Mr. Fox came prowling,
　　Sandy had a twinge of fear!
Hid behind a sturdy tree-trunk,
　　Cocked a timid little ear!

Saw him tearing up the notice,

    Felt a sudden, awful fright:

Sandy's heart went pitter-patter,

    And he bolted out of sight!

Mr. Fox went prowling further
On his rabbit hunting way.
Bobbity appeared, and Sandy
Came out eagerly to play.

Bobbity said " Hello, Sandy !
   Would you like to come with me
To the Woodland Picnic Party ?
   Here's a notice on the tree ! "

Hand-in-hand they went together
   Through the leafy sunlit wood :
Sandy's nervousness had vanished
   And he thought " This will be good ! "

Now, a Woodland Picnic Party
Was a *very special* thing:
Woodland Mice and Woodland Rabbits
Gathered round to dance and sing.

Round the mighty Toadstool Table,
Underneath a leafy sky,
While they gazed upon the banquet
—Apples, carrots, bramble pie!

Then at last the guests were seated:

Woodland Rabbits, Woodland Mice,

Fell upon the feast with gusto:

No-one had to ask them twice!

Cherries, acorns, lettuce vanished

In the twinkling of an eye!

No-one noticed wily Foxey,

On the scent, and lurking by!

Silently he padded forward:

    Owlie, from his Hole-in-Tree,

Saw him, so he called a warning,

    " Too-whit-too-whoo-whoo-whoo ! "
                                   went he.

At that sudden startling signal

    All the Woodland Folk, in fright,

Disappeared below the table,

    Shrank together, out of sight.

Very still and very silent,

    Listening for the slightest sound:

Then—they scarcely heard a rustle—

    Wily Fox came sniffing round.

Saw the now deserted table

With a glistening, greedy eye.

Then, with many a grunt and gurgle,

Sat and ate the bramble pie!

Then old Foxey, full and drowsy,

    Dropped his head and fell asleep:

When he heard him, faintly snoring,

    Sandy just risked one peep!

Whispered softly to the others,

    " Foxey's sleeping ! Not a sound ! "

Out they came, in breathless silence,

    Crept a-tiptoe, homeward bound !

Once around the nearest tree-trunk,

Off they fled, in anxious haste :

Would old Foxey wake and see them ?

Owl cried " Noooo ! " and on they raced !

So, at last, they reached the warren,

    Bolted quickly down below:

Bobbity was first, then Sandy!

    Safe where Foxey couldn't go!

Bobbity had lit the lantern,
    Sandy caught his breath again:
So they finished tea in comfort,
    Snug and safe, down Rabbit Lane!

Sandy's mind went back to Michael
    And the empty rabbit hutch,
And he felt a little sorry,
    Michael wouldn't like it much!

For he didn't know that Michael
    Found another rabbit pet,
Black and white, and very friendly!
    . . . And he doesn't know it yet!